Roger Hurn used to be an actor in 'The 'Exploding Trouser Company'. He has also appeared on 'The Weakest Link' on TV – and he won!

Now he spends his time writing and telling stories. His scariest and spookiest experience came when he went to an old ghost town in the Wild West of the USA. This gave him the idea for **Spook Squad.**

He hopes you enjoy reading the Spook Squad's adventures as much as he enjoyed writing them.

Spook Squad
Danger in Dead Man's Lane
by Roger Hurn
Illustrated by Peter Richardson

Published by Ransom Publishing Ltd.
Radley House, 8 St. Cross Road, Winchester, Hampshire
SO23 9HX, UK
www.ransom.co.uk

ISBN 978 184167 074 4
First published in 2012

A CIP catalogue record of this book is available from the British Library.

SPOOK SQUAD

Danger

in

Dead Man's Lane

by Roger Hurn

Ransom

DEAD END JUNCTION

Vlad the Bad's Castle

THE GHOST TRAIN RAILWAY

GHOULS' GRAVEYARD

THE ISLE OF FRIGHT

It's the dead centre of Otherworld!

THE WRAITH PITS
They really are the pits!

THE HAUNTED PYRAMID
Your mummy warned you about this place

HERE THERE BE DRAGONS

BANSHEE BAY
Where the wind never stops howling!

They sleep in the day and fight knights!

Otherworld

GOBLIN GULCH
The home of
messy eaters

FANG MOUNTAINS
You'll say 'Fangs for
nothing' if you try to
climb them

**KRAKEN
LAKE**

Swim at
your
own risk!

SPOOK CITY

THE ZOMBI RIVER

WEREWOLF WOODS
Avoid when the
moon is full!

Otherworld

Where is Otherworld?

The far side of a shadow.

Who lives there?

Ghouls, ghosts, long-leggedy beasties and things that go bump in the night.

Why do the creatures who live there come to our world?

To make mischief.

Rhee the Banshee answers readers' questions.

How do they get here?

> They slip through secret gateways
> when you're not looking.

Can humans go to Otherworld?

> Yes, but they shouldn't.

Why not?

> Because they never come back.

Why not?

> Trust me – you really
> **DO NOT** want to know!

7

Meet The SPOOK SQUAD

Emma

FYI: She spends her life getting hold of the wrong end of the stick.

Loves: Getting the point.

Hates: Muddy sticks.

Fact: She doesn't like vampires – she thinks they're a pain in the neck.

Roxy

FYI: Don't call her 'Ginger' – unless you want to eat your dinner through a straw.

Loves: Being a strawberry blonde.

Hates: Seeing red.

Fact: She reckons cannibal goblins are messy eaters, so she won't be joining their fang club.

Nita

FYI: This girl gets gadgets. Give her a paper clip, a rubber band, a tin can and an A4 battery and she'll rig up a gizmo that'll blow your gran's pop socks off.

Loves: Fixing things.

Hates: Fixing it – if it ain't broke.

Fact: Nita has invented ghost-proof wheels for her bike. They don't have any spooks!

Leena

FYI: If she was any sharper you could use her to slice bread.

Loves: Big words.

Hates: Small minds.

Fact: She prefers whatwolves and whenwolves to werewolves.

Aunt Rhee

FYI: Rhee's not the kind of aunt who gives you a woolly jumper for Christmas.

Loves: Walking on the wild side.

Hates: Things that go bump in the night.

Fact: Rhee is just too cool for ghouls.

Rattle

FYI: Rattle says he's a poltergeist. He thinks poltergeists are posher than ghosts.

Loves: Boo-berry pie and I-scream.

Hates: People who sneak up behind him and shout BOO!

Fact: Rattle's only happy when he's moaning.

Interview with Leena

The Spook Squad's Leena answers readers' questions.

What's the best thing about being in the Spook Squad?

> We get to spook the spooks. Try saying that quickly ten times!

Have you ever made friends with a ghost?

> Yes, but it didn't last.

Why not?

> It didn't believe in people.

Which is your favourite Spook Squad adventure?

> Ghouls in School.

Why?

> Because I throw a dish of custard at Mr Bull, our headteacher – and I don't get into trouble for doing it!

The Shape-shifter

Description:
It looks like anything it wants to be.

Strength:
Never has a bad hair day.

Weakness: It's a bit two-faced.

Likes: Getting a shift on.

Dislikes: Getting stuck in a rut.

Favourite game: Charades.

Scream Scale Rating:
It all depends on what it's being!

CREATURE
FEATURE

Chapter One

Danger in
Dead Man's Lane

It was dusk and the sun was sinking behind the trees on Dead Man's Lane.

Roxy, Leena and Emma were on their way to Aunt Rhee's house. They were going to watch their favourite DVD: *Ghouldelocks and the Three Scares*. Nita was at after-school science club. She was going to come over later.

Roxy heard a snuffling sound behind her.

She spun round and saw a large, ugly-looking dog sneaking up on her.

'What's up, Rox?' asked Leena.

Roxy pointed. 'That dog. It's spooking me.'

The girls stared at the dog. It stared back at them.

'Well, it's not going to win the *Prettiest dog in show* prize at Cruft's any time soon,' said Leena. 'But I guess it's harmless.'

The dog blinked. It looked offended.

Roxy shrugged. 'OK,' she said. 'But let's get to Rhee's house before it gets too dark.'

The Spook Squad hurried on. Roxy glanced back over her shoulder. The dog was loping after them. It was not wagging its tail.

'Hey, guys,' said Roxy. 'That dog is following us.'

The girls turned to look, but the dog had vanished into thin air.

'I don't like this,' said Emma.

'Me neither,' said Leena.

'Hey you lot, get a grip,' said Roxy. 'Remember, the Spook Squad does not know the meaning of the word *fear*.'

'That's true,' said Leena. 'But there are lots of words we don't know the meaning of.'

Suddenly the Spook Squad was startled by a noise from above their heads. They looked up. There on a tree branch was a

huge crow. They could see themselves reflected in its hard, black eye.

'Hello Spook Squad,' it cawed. 'What's a nice bunch of girls like you doing in a lonely place like this?'

Chapter Two

Shaping Up

'Hey,' said Roxy. 'You *were* the dog – but now you're a crow! Are you a shape-shifter?'

'No. I'm a dog going to a fancy dress party in a crow costume,' said the crow.

It flapped its wings and swooped down to the road. Then it disappeared in a flurry of feathers, and in its place stood a tough-looking man with a huge beak of a nose.

The man glared at the girls. 'Of course

I'm a shape-shifter.'

'So what do you want with us?' asked Emma.

The shape-shifter's eyes glittered like two chips of ice. 'Well,' he said. 'Back home in Otherworld, you girls are as popular as a skunk with the squits.'

'We try,' said Leena.

The shape-shifter ignored her. 'So the ghouls, the ghosts, the long-leggedy beasties, the goblins, trolls and vampires had a meeting and decided they are fed up to the back fangs with you lot meddling in their business.'

'Wow! That was some meeting,' said Roxy. 'Where did they hold it – the Vampire State Building?'

The shape-shifter's eyes glowed red.

'Oh very funny,' he snarled. 'Now laugh this off. They've sent me – a shape-shifting bounty hunter – to put an end to the Spook Squad once and for all!'

The girls gulped.

'Er … if you're a bounty hunter, that means there's a price on our heads,' said Roxy.

The shape-shifter nodded. 'Yes, but I've got to take your heads back to Otherworld before I get the gold. And, as they are still on your necks, I'm going to have to twist them off!'

Chapter Three

A Jumbo Challenge

Nita came hurtling down Dead Man's Lane. She skidded to a halt next to the shape-shifter.

'I'm Nita,' she said. 'Who are you?'

'He's a shape-shifter,' said Roxy.

'Wow,' said Nita. 'Can I see you shape-shift?'

'No,' said the shape-shifter. 'I'm busy.

I've got to twist all your heads off.'

'Oh don't be such a grouch,' said Roxy. *'We've* seen you in action – but Nita hasn't.'

'That's right,' said Emma.

'So why don't you stop trying to twist our heads off and show her?' said Leena.

The shape-shifter frowned. 'Well, I don't know … ' he said.

'Oh come on,' said Nita. 'Turn yourself into something amazing.'

Leena laughed. 'He can't do *amazing*. He can only do dogs and crows.'

The shape-shifter shook his fist at her. 'I'll show you amazing,' he shouted. 'Watch this!'

The shape-shifter trembled and shook

and then began to grow bigger. Before the Spook Squad's eyes he changed into an elephant. The elephant trumpeted and then changed back into human shape.

'Was that amazing enough for you?' he asked.

Nita shrugged. 'The ears were too small for an elephant,' she said.

'That's because I was an Indian elephant,' said the shape-shifter. 'They have smaller ears than African elephants. It's a well-known fact.'

'If you say so,' said Nita.

'I do,' said the shape-shifter. 'Anyway, now it's time I pulled off all your heads and put them in a sack.'

'But you haven't got a sack,' said Emma.

The shape-shifter grinned. He pulled out a small bag from his back pocket.

'Huh,' said Leena. 'That bag's way too

small. You'll never get all our heads in there!'

The shape-shifter shook the sack. To the Spook Squad's horror, it expanded like an air bag in a car.

'Oh, I think I will,' he said.

Chapter Four

Spiderphobia

Things were looking bad for the Spook Squad. The shape-shifter snarled and moved towards them. All the girls backed away – except Nita. She folded her arms, pursed her lips and tapped her foot. She looked like a teacher about to marmalise a naughty child.

'It is a well-known fact that any old shape-shifter can do big,' she said. 'But are you clever enough to do *tiny*?'

The shape-shifter stopped. 'Of course I am,' he sneered.

'Then prove it!' snapped Nita.

He sighed and put the sack back in his pocket. 'OK. What sort of tiny creature do you want?'

'Oh, anything but a spider,' squealed Emma. 'I am *soooo* scared of spiders. Please don't change into one of those horrible hairy ones. I'll scream if you do.'

'So will I,' said Roxy. 'Please, *please*, PLEASE don't turn into a spider.'

'Oh yes,' said Leena, 'I'd rather have my head pulled off and put in a sack than have a spider crawl all over me.'

The girls clung to each other. Emma burst into tears.

The shape-shifter rubbed his hands together with glee. 'Sorry girls, but a horrible hairy spider it is. Get ready to scream!'

The shape-shifter's body shrunk down until it was a round, fat little ball. Then it sprouted eight hairy legs. It waved the front two at the Spook Squad.

Instead of screaming, Nita pulled a jar from her school bag. She scooped the spider up into it. Then she slammed the lid on the top of the jar.

'Gotcha!' she yelled.

Chapter Five

The Big Picture

The Spook Squad stared at the spider in the jar. It wasn't moving.

'I hope you haven't killed it,' said Emma.

Nita shook her head. 'Don't worry, Em. This jar has got a special chemical in it which puts insects to sleep, so I can study them.'

'*Riiight*,' said Roxy. 'So Incy Wincy spider here is out for the count, is he?'

Nita shook her head. 'No, he'll wake up soon.'

Roxy did not look happy. 'Brilliant,' she said. 'So what do we do then?'

Just then the air popped and Rattle the poltergeist appeared. 'Oh here you are,' he said. 'Rhee sent me to find you. You're late for your tea.'

He saw the spider in Nita's jar. 'What's that?' he said.

'A double-decker bus,' snapped Roxy. 'What does it look like?'

Rattle peered at the jar. 'It looks like an ugly bug,' he said. 'Urghhh – it makes my flesh creep!'

'But you haven't got any flesh,' said Nita. 'You're a ghost.'

'Don't be so ghostist,' said Rattle. He vanished into thin air, then suddenly reappeared. 'And don't even *think* of bringing that spider thing home with you,' he snapped, before vanishing again.

'Hey, Rattle's given me an idea,' said Nita. 'Let's take the shape-shifter to Rhee.

She'll know what to do with him.'

'OK,' said Leena. 'But we'd better get a shift on. Spiderman's going to be waking up soon.'

The girls raced off down the lane to Rhee's house.

Rhee's plan was simple. First, she took a photo of the Spook Squad holding the jar with the spider. They looked like big game hunters with a trophy.

· · · · ·

When the shape-shifter woke up and changed back, he found himself face to face with an angry banshee.

'You've failed, Mr Shifter' she said. 'So sneak off back into Otherworld and never show your ugly face here again.'

'O.K.,' he snarled. 'You've won this time – but I'll be back soon.'

'No, you won't,' said Rhee. 'Because if you do, I'll tell everyone in Otherworld how the mighty shape-shifting bounty hunter was trapped in a jar by a bunch of girls.'

The shape-shifter laughed. 'They'll never believe you,' he said.

Rhee smiled a smile as cold as an ice cube in a deep freeze. 'Oh I think they will when they see this photo on the cover of *Hallo-ween* magazine.'

She thrust the picture she had taken under the shape-shifter's nose. 'Get the picture?'

He looked at it in horror. 'No, please – I'm begging you,' sobbed the shape-shifter. 'My mum reads that.'

'So scram,' said Rhee, 'and *never* come back!'

Roxy pulled out a camera. 'Hey, Spiderman, how about one last photo with the Spook Squad?' she said. 'We'll even sign it for you, won't we guys?'

The shape-shifter screamed and fled.

'Oh dear,' said Emma. 'He's gone all camera shy.'

'Never mind,' said Roxy. 'With a face like his, he would only have broken the camera anyway!'

The next Spook Squad adventure is

Things That Go Bump in the Night

It's a Scream!

Spook Squad's Scary Joke Page

Where do ghost trains stop?

At devil crossings!

Did you hear about the woman who married a ghost?

Yes. I don't know what possessed her!

Why did the boy go out with a clock and a canary on Halloween night?

He was playing 'tick or tweet'!